LATE ELEMENTARY PIANO

FUN & GAMES
for Christmas

By Wynn-Anne Rossi

D1603930

Production: Frank and Gail Hackinson
Production Coordinator: Philip Gröeber
Editors: Elizabeth Gutierrez and Edwin McLean
Cover: Susan Schutt-Bruhn
Typography & Illustrations: Susan Schutt-Bruhn
Engraving: Tempo Music Press, Inc.
Printer: Tempo Music Press, Inc.

THE
F·J·H
MUSIC
COMPANY
INC.

A Note to Teachers

Fun & Games for Christmas is a playful way to musically celebrate the Christmas season. Following in the footsteps of **Fun & Games, Books One and Two**, it is a collection of humorous pieces with unusual challenges coupled with zany piano games that teach important musical concepts. The emphasis is on motivation and the natural friendship that can develop with the instrument.

Special directions are found throughout the pieces involving everything from stomping the feet to improvising on the black keys. Holiday games involve musical markings, sight-reading skills, and creative rhythms. Students will enjoy exploring new boundaries of what music can be while celebrating the season.

It is suggested that these pieces be saved for the end of each daily practice. This book can serve as an effective reward for work at the piano and will help the students leave their practice sessions with plenty of "Christmas spirit."

Contents

Oh, the Christmas Tree

Keeps Falling Over

Traditional
(adapted)

* For easy gliding, stroke the keys lightly on the fingerpads, with wrists high.

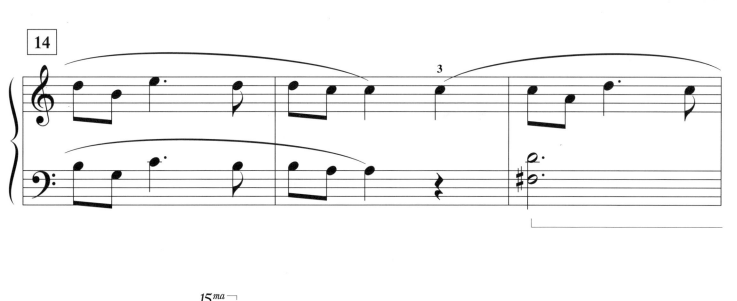

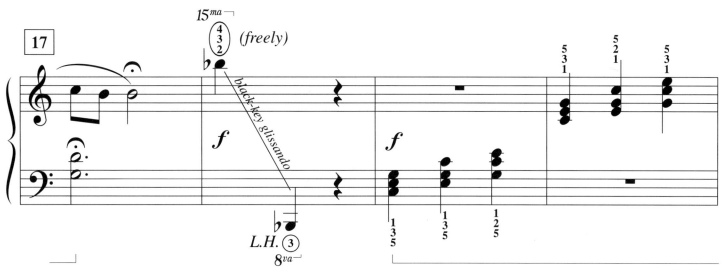

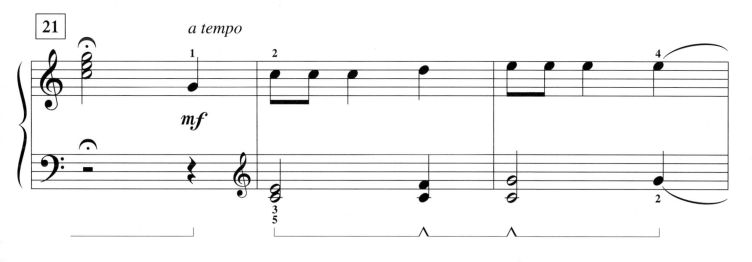

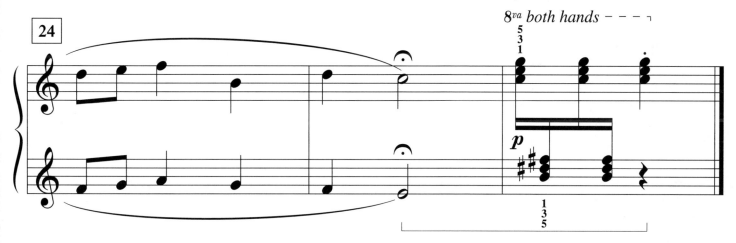

Deck the Hall

with Loads of 8th Notes

Traditional
(adapted)

Stomp Your Hooves to Reindeer Rhythms

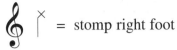 = stomp right foot

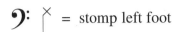 = stomp left foot

While seated, stomp each reindeer rhythm below and discover a familiar Christmas carol. Write the name of the carol in each blank.

Name: _____

Name: _____

Name: _____

Write your own reindeer rhythm below.

Jolly Ol' St. Nicholas

Ate Too Much Plum Pudding

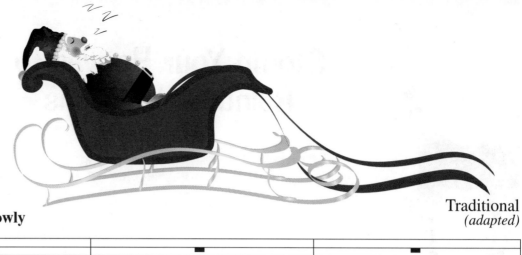

Traditional
(adapted)

Heavily and very slowly

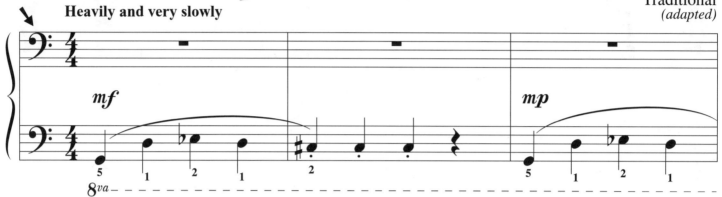

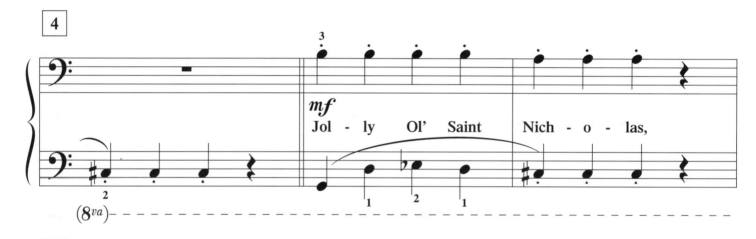

Jol - ly Ol' Saint Nich - o - las,

in his com - fy chair,

Ate his pud - ding

to the last with a sweet - ened pear.

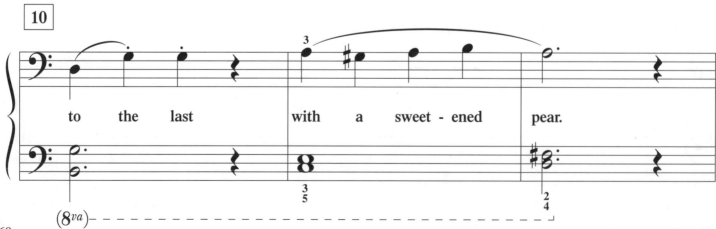

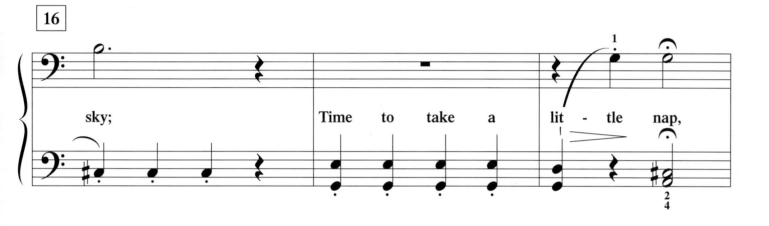

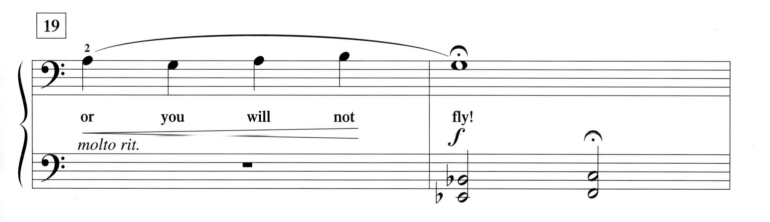

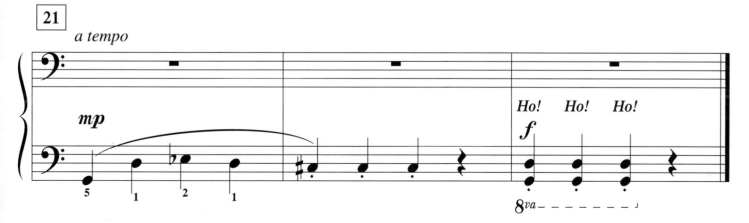

Jingle Bells Everywhere

= Play clusters of black keys high on the keyboard. Notice that all notes in this piece are flatted, except F!

J. Pierpont
(adapted)

Joyfully

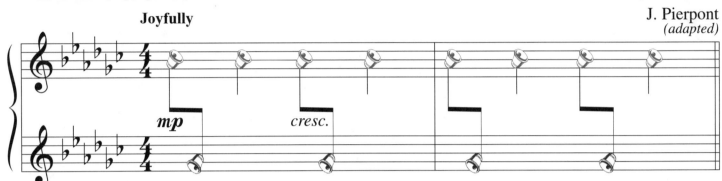

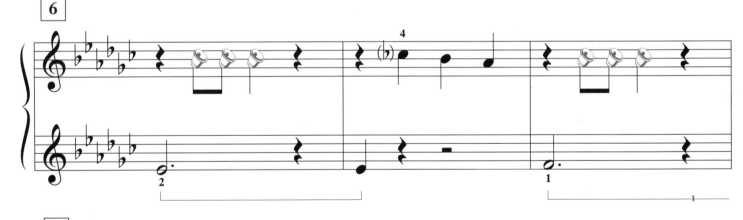

(L.H. cross over)

12

Fun with "Ho! Ho! Ho!"

Match the following dynamic signs and articulations to their correct definitions.

Use them to create a different "Ho! Ho! Ho!" sound for each picture below. (The first one is done for you.)

Then say each one for your teacher!

	staccato	play this note louder
(cresc.)	cresc.	smooth and connected
mf	mezzo forte	loud
mp	mezzo piano	growing louder
	dim.	detached and separated
	accent	medium loud
p	piano	medium soft
	legato	becoming softer
f	forte	soft

HO HO HO

HO HO HO

HO HO HO

HO HO HO

Reindeer Play
Up on the Housetop

Benjamin R. Hanby
(adapted)

With a sense of humor

Vibrate your lips for a reindeer noise.

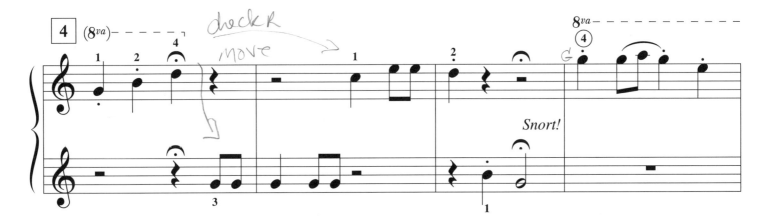

Snort!

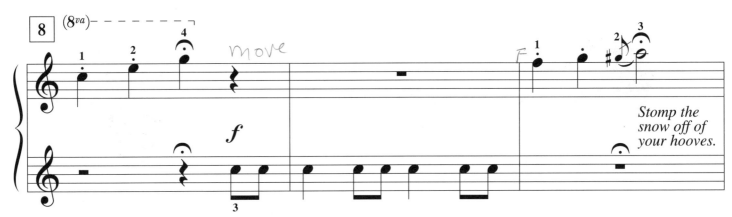

Stomp the snow off of your hooves.

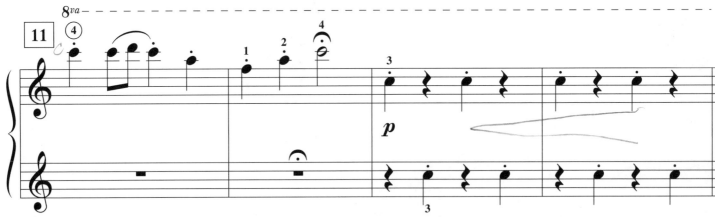

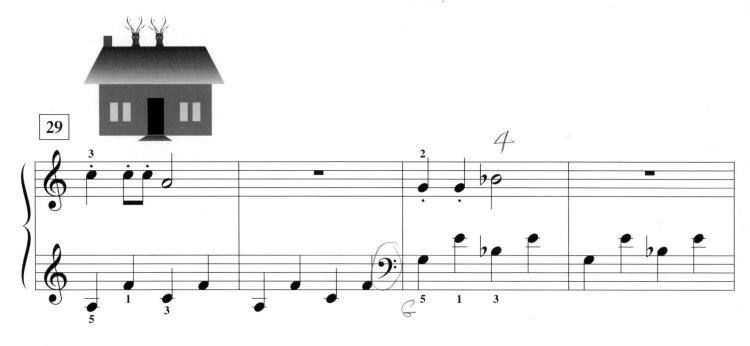

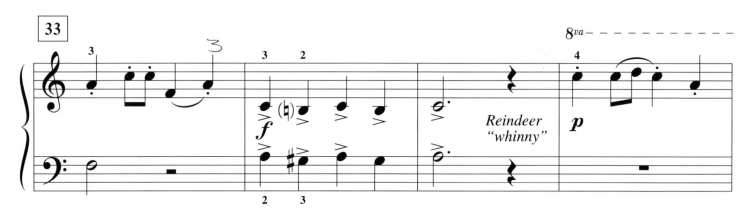

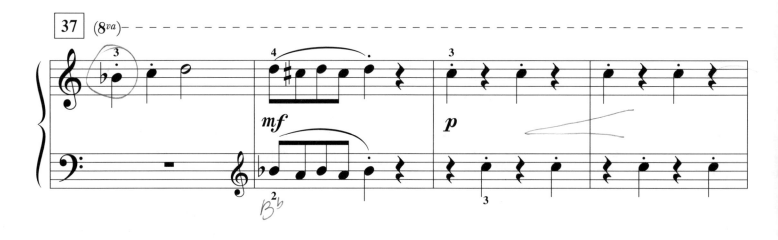

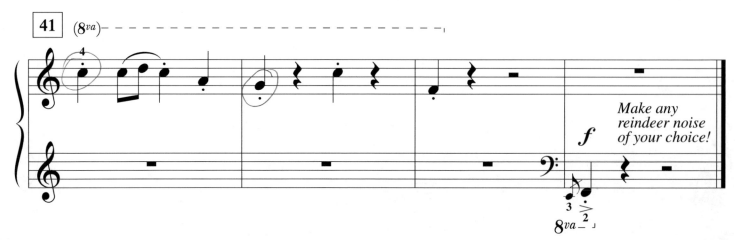

Open Your Matching Gifts!

Match each gift on the left with the correct gift on
the right to complete a familiar Christmas tune.

Then play each one without pause.

Can you name each tune? (Answers below)

18

We Wish You A Very Merry Christmas
with a Sad Case of Candy Hiccups!

= knock on the wood of the piano

With holiday cheer

Traditional
(adapted)

We wish you a ver-y mer-ry
mf

Christ-mas; *(hiccup)* We wish you a ver-y mer-ry Christ-mas. *(hiccup)* We

wish you a ver-y mer-ry Christ-mas *(hiccup)* and a Hap-py New

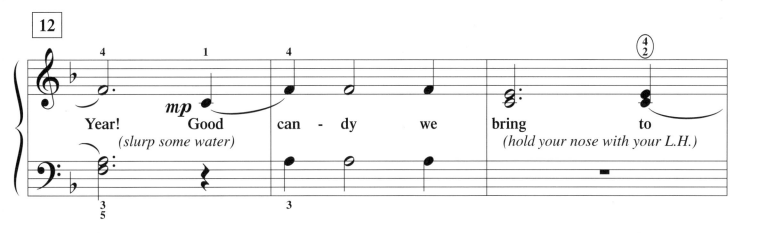

12

Year! Good can - dy we bring to
(slurp some water) *(hold your nose with your L.H.)*

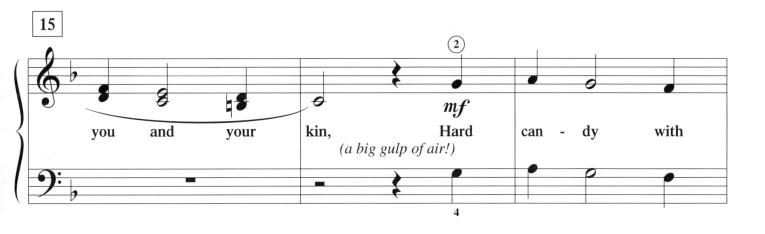

15

you and your kin, Hard can - dy with
(a big gulp of air!)

D.S. 𝄋 al Coda

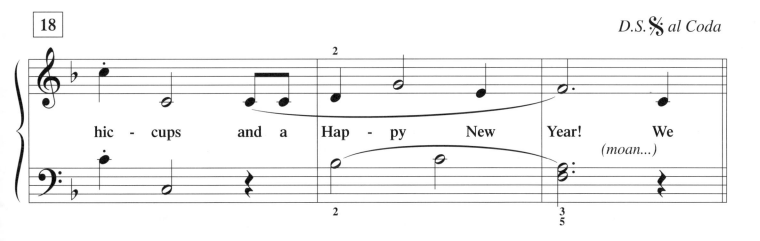

18

hic - cups and a Hap - py New Year! We
(moan...)

Coda

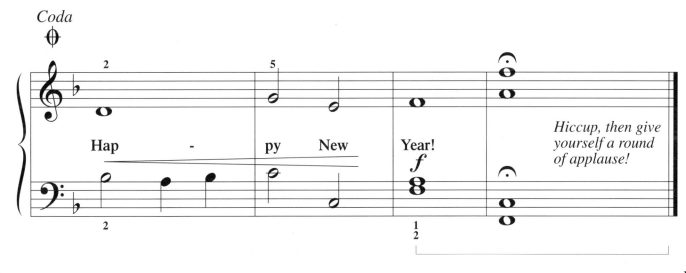

Hap - py New Year!

Hiccup, then give yourself a round of applause!

FF1269

Decorate the Music Tree

Using the color key, color each ornament below. Keep decorating by drawing other music notes and symbols on the tree. (See page 13 for ideas.)

A = red   C = yellow   E = blue   G = pink
B = orange   D = green   F = purple

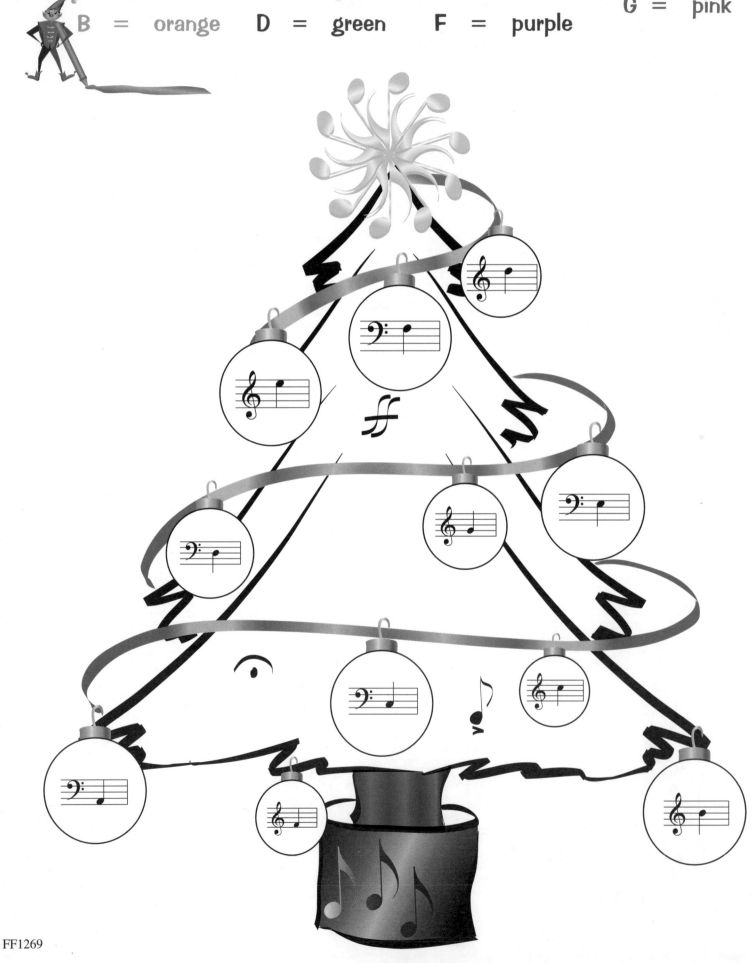